WELCOME TO THE WORLD OF Geronimo Stilton

GERONIMO
STILTON

Published by Sweet Cherry Publishing Limited
Unit 36, Vulcan House,
Vulcan Road,
Leicester, LE5 3EF
United Kingdom

First published in the UK in 2021
2021 edition

2 4 6 8 10 9 7 5 3 1

ISBN: 978-1-78226-806-2

Text by Geronimo Stilton
Art Director: Iacopo Bruno
Graphic Designer: Andrea Cavallini / theWorldofDOT
Original cover illustration by Andrea Da Rold and Andrea Cavallini
Concept of illustration by Lorenzo Chiavini and Roberto Ronchi.
Artistic coordination by Gògo Gó in collaboration with Certosina Kashmir
Initial and final page illustrations by Roberto Ronchi and Ennio Bufi MAD5, Studio Parlapà and Andrea Cavallini. Map illustrations by Andrea Da Rold and Andrea Cavallini
Cover layout and typography by Dominika Plocka
Interior layout and typography by Dominika Plocka
Graphics by Merenguita Gingermouse and Zeppola Zap

Original title: Quattro topi nel far west!
Based on an original idea by Elisabetta Dami

www.geronimostilton.com/uk

www.sweetcherrypublishing.com

Printed and bound in Turkey
T.OP005

Geronimo Stilton

THE WILD, WILD WEST

Sweet Cherry

They Say I'm a Scaredy-Mouse

Do you know me? My name is Stilton, **Geronimo Stilton**.

I am the editor of the most popular paper in New Mouse City. It's called *The Rodent's Gazette*. Most mice would agree, I'm a pretty **BRAINY** rodent. And I absolutely love to read.

After a hard day at the office, I like to relax in my **cosy** mouse hole. I slip into my fluffy cat-fur slippers. Then I settle down with a good book in front of the fireplace.

I make myself a nice cup of hot Cheddar tea. **Yum!** And sometimes I put on some soft music.

Oh, what a perfect way ...

... to escape from the rat race.

Of course, some rodents might say I am a little on the **boring** side. Like my sister Thea and my cousin Trap. They make fun of me because I don't like to travel. They say I'm a SCAREDY-MOUSE. You see, I am not the adventurous type. But that is because ...

... I get **SEASICK**

... heights make me **dizzy**

... and I'm a *worrywart!*

Now, you are probably wondering what I am doing in this adventure. It takes place in the **WILD, WILD WEST**. Out West you will find sun-scorched deserts, raging bulls, and even poisonous snakes.

Why would I, Geronimo "*Scaredy-Mouse*" Stilton, travel to a place like that?

Read this book and you'll understand ....

HERE IS THE MAP OF NORTH AMERICA.

DO YOU KNOW WHERE
THE **WILD, WILD WEST** IS?

THE WILD WEST AND THE NATIVE AMERICANS

The term Wild West began to be used in the 1800s to describe the regions of the Great Plains and the Rocky Mountains, which extend west of the Mississippi River to the coast of the Pacific Ocean. Many Native American tribes inhabited these immense territories. Here are the better-known ones:

APACHE: A group of communities (Mescalero, San Carlos, Fort Apache, Apache Peaks, Mazatzal, and others) that share the same language. Famous chiefs include Geronimo and Cochise.

BLACKFOOT: A community who now live in Montana and parts of Canada, the Blackfoot Nation were famous for their shoemaking ability. The Blackfoot dyed their moccasins black.

CHEROKEE: A community in Tennessee and North Carolina. A Cherokee leader, Sequoya, invented an alphabet for the Cherokee language that was made up of eighty-five symbols.

CHEYENNE: A community based in Montana and Oklahoma, the Cheyenne once lived in tepees made from long poles and buffalo skins. They were skilled buffalo hunters.

COMANCHE: A community based in Oklahoma, the Comanche originate from the Great Plains, where they were known as skilled horsemen.

SIOUX: A group of communities, also known as the Lakota. Sitting Bull, Crazy Horse, and Red Cloud were famous Sioux chiefs.

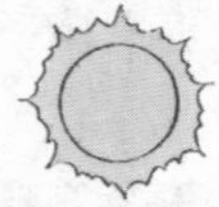

Four Mice in the Wild West

It was **HOT**.

It was dry.

It was a bad, bad fur day. Even my tail was sweating.

Oh, what I wouldn't give for a cold Cheddar ice pop from my mega-huge fridge. Too bad I couldn't get one. Do you want to know why?

Because I was in the **ARIZONA DESERT**.

Yes, mouse fans, I, Geronimo Stilton, was in the

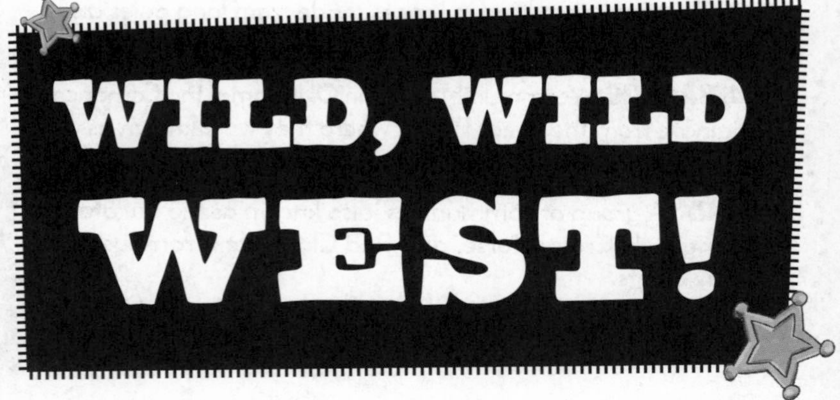

Lucky for me, I wasn't **alone**. My sister Thea, my cousin Trap, and my little nephew Benjamin were with me. Together, we were crossing the scorching desert.

Have you ever been to a desert? There is not much to see. Just **sand**, **rocks** and **cacti**.

The sand burned my paws. I kept tripping over the rocks. And my tail was getting ripped to shreds on all those pointy cactus needles. **Ouch!**

Worst of all, I was dying of thirst. I shook my canteen. It was empty.

Just then a dark shadow fell over me. I gulped. Something told me it wasn't Santa Mouse flying by on his way to his summer place. I looked up.

RANCID RAT HAIRS! It was a hungry pack of vultures waiting to lick our bones.

This place was a total nightmare!

Aaagh!
Aaagh!
Aaagh!
Aaagh!

Welcome to Cactus City!

After a **BILLION YEARS**, we finally reached a dusty set of railway tracks.

CHEESECAKE! We were saved! The tracks led us to a wooden sign. In big letters it read:

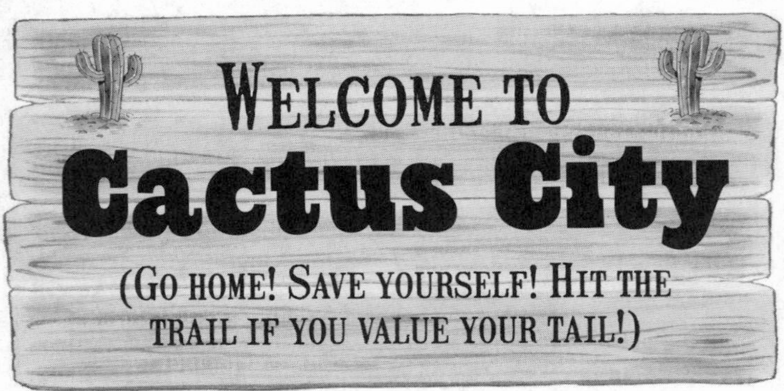

I twisted my tail up in knots. "Uh-oh," I gulped. "This doesn't look good. This doesn't look good at all. In fact, this looks downright **BAD**, if you ask me."

Trap pushed me forward. "Oh, don't be such a scaredy-mouse, **Germeister**," he snorted. He gave me another shove.

I tumbled head first into a cactus. "**Don't push me!** I can't stand it when you push me!" I yelled, picking needles out of my fur.

Have I told you my cousin Trap is the most annoying rodent on the planet?

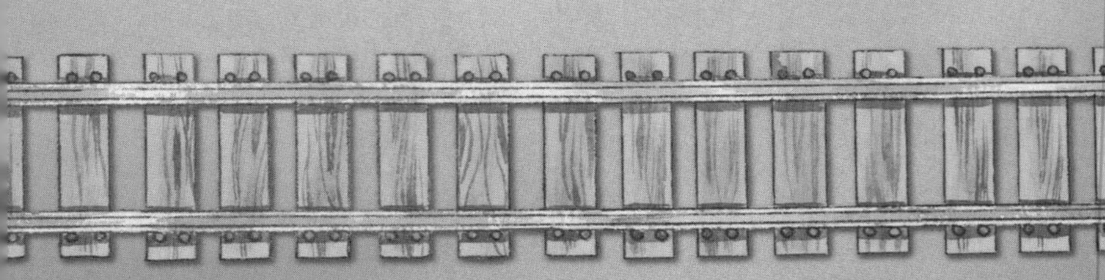

TRADING POST
Cactus City

SALOON
SALOON
SHERIFF
JAIL

Cactus City

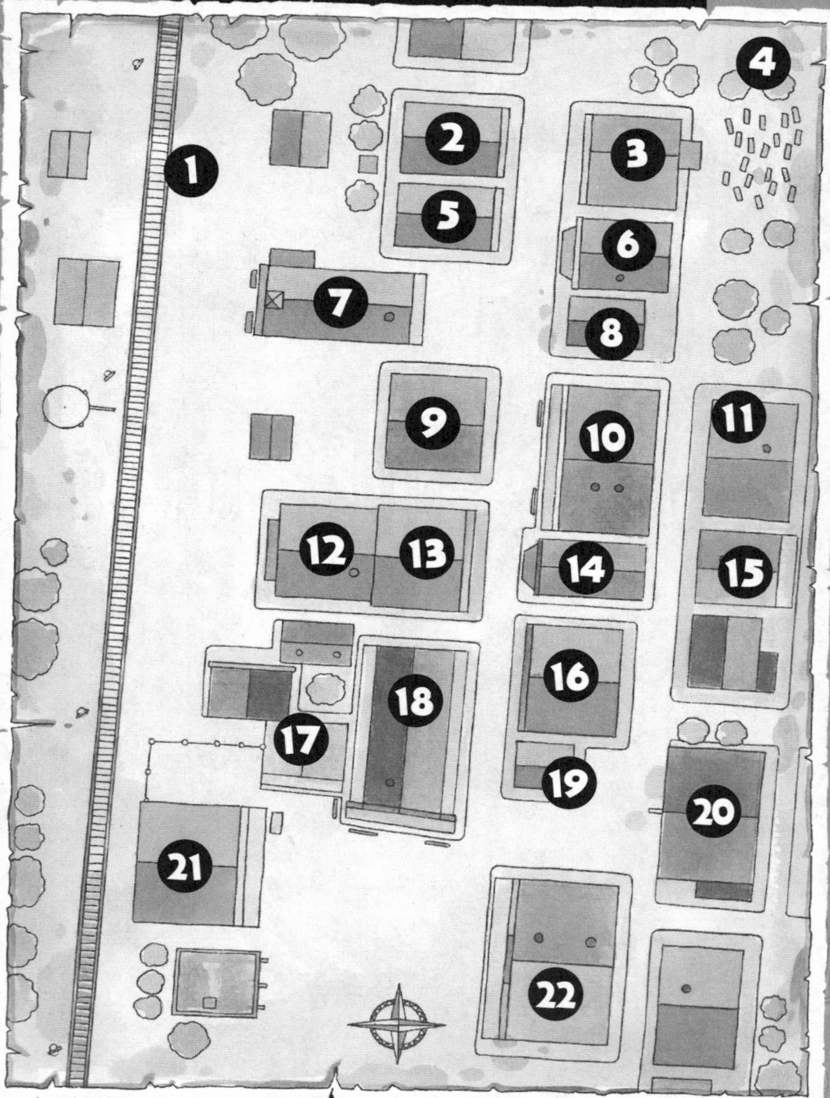

MAP OF Cactus City

1. RAILWAY
2. LAWYER
3. UNDERTAKER
4. CEMETERY
5. COURTHOUSE
6. DRESS SHOP
7. BARN
8. BLACKSMITH
9. GENERAL STORE
10. SALOON
11. SCHOOL
12. RAILWAY STATION
13. DEPOT
14. PRINTER
15. SCHOOLTEACHER'S HOUSE
16. SHERIFF
17. TRADING POST
18. BANK
19. JAIL
20. DOCTOR'S HOUSE
21. HOTEL
22. HOSPITAL

The Law in the Wild West

At first, no one was concerned with the public order in the towns of the Wild West. Then the government of the United States sent sheriffs and judges to keep order and to enforce the law.

What's Wrong with Cactus City?

A wiry old mouse stood in front of the railway station. He was dressed in a uniform.

"**Howdy**, strangers, what brings you to Cactus City?" he called, waving us over. "The name's CHOO-CHOO CHEDDAR, that's C.C. for short," he chattered. "I lend a paw down here at the station. Yep, been working here for some **twenty years**. I sell tickets, carry bags. Yep, you name it, I've done it. Sometimes I even ..."

CHOO-CHOO CHEDDAR
The Stationmaster

Suddenly C.C. stopped mid-sentence. I noticed he was staring at us with an odd expression on his snout.

"Well, **GOLLY**," he cried. "You mouselings must have come from way far off yonder. Just look at your duds. Shucks, you're dressed just like city mice."

C.C. offered us some **stewed beans** and a sip of water.

"Sorry I can't get you more to drink," he said in a low voice. "Water is hard to come by in these parts." He looked around nervously. Then he whispered, "Let me give you some advice, strangers. Get out of town now!"

HOW STRANGE. What was wrong with Cactus City? It looked like a nice little town to me.

I was still thinking about C.C.'s words when a train rumbled into the station.

A rat with **LONG**, waxed whiskers got off. It was CURLY, the train conductor.

"Cactus City! Last station before the desert!" he yelled.

CURLY
The Train Condu

No one got off the train. No one stopped in Cactus City.

HOW STRANGE. What was wrong with Cactus City?

We decided to check out the town.

First we passed the blacksmith's shop. A **HUGE MUSCLEMOUSE** was hammering away on a piece of metal. He was making a horseshoe.

A mouse carrying a **doctor's bag** scampered by. "Clear the way!" he squeaked. "Nancy Nibbler's about to have those triplets! "

A plump mouse stuck his head out of a building door. It was the **banker**. He looked around nervously. Then he raced back inside.

I wondered why he looked so worried.

Just then I heard a familiar noise. It was a **PRINTING PRESS!**

A rat with tiny glasses was busy **PRINTING** the newspaper. He glanced up at us suspiciously.

We passed by a courthouse. An old **JUDGE** peeked out the door. He looked around. Then he slammed the door shut.

In front of the **SALOON**, a rodent sat in a rocking chair. A big hat covered his face. He stopped rocking when we walked by. ***HOW ODD***. I thought he was napping. But it seemed as if he were hiding from something.

TOMMY
The Printer

MORRIS
The Judge

Minutes later, we ran into the **UNDERTAKER**. He shook our paws warmly.

He had a huge **GRIN** plastered on his face. *At least one rodent wasn't worried,* I thought.

"Welcome to Cactus City, strangers!" The undertaker **beamed**. "If I can be of service, don't be shy. Today I'm having a two-for-one special. Yessiree, that's two stiffs for the price of one!"

A buck-toothed rodent stood next to him. He held up a shovel. I guessed he was a **gravedigger**.

"Just tell me how deep and I'll dig it!"

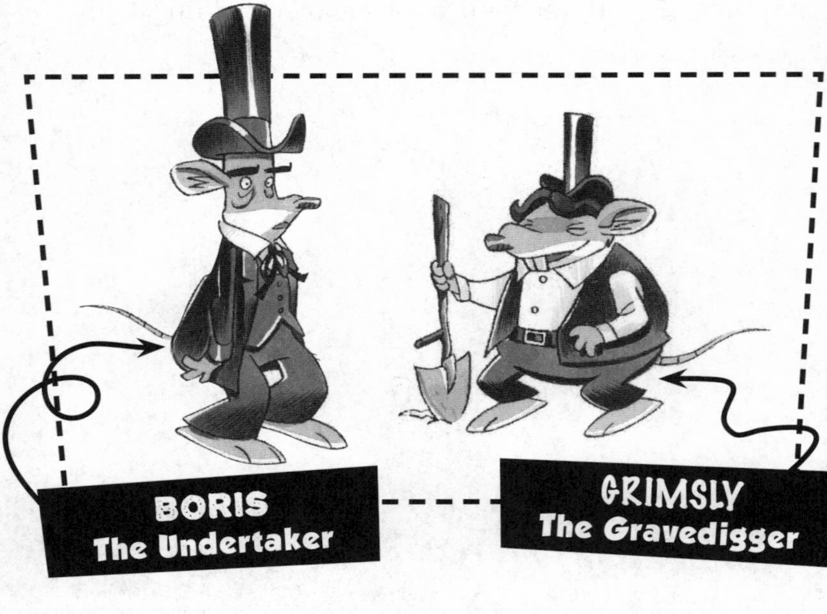

BORIS
The Undertaker

GRIMSLY
The Gravedigger

I *shivered*. Then I noticed something else that was strange about Cactus City.

There was no **sheriff**. Do you know what a sheriff does? He keeps order in the town. He locks up bad rodents in his jail. Sort of like the **Chief of Police** in New Mouse City.

If My Friends Could See Me Now

We found the general store in the centre of town. Inside, a short, stocky mouse greeted us.

"Howdy, strangers! Welcome to **Blunt Rat Bob's**," he squeaked. "Bob's the name. Stuff is my game. And, strangers, do you look like you need some stuff! Those duds you're wearing look **ridiculous!**"

I stared down at my suit. I guess I did look out of place. But ridiculous? No way.

Blunt Rat Bob
The General Store Owner

Meanwhile, Bob had run off. He returned a few minutes later with a pawful of clothes.

I pulled on a pair of leather trousers, boots with **SPURS**, a checked shirt, and a cowrat hat. Then I looked at myself in the mirror. I must admit, I looked pretty cool. I felt just like a **REAL COWRAT**. "If only my friends at *The Rodent's Gazette* could see me now."

My family seemed just as excited.

Benjamin jumped up and down. "If only my friends at school could see me now!" he exclaimed.

Trap wiggled his tail. "If only my friends down at the **Squeak and Chew** could see me now," he chuckled.

Thea winked at her own reflection. Then she tried to take a step. She tried to jump. She tried to run. But her dress was so long she couldn't move. Instead, she **fell flat on her snout!**

"Thank goodness my friends can't see me now," she snorted. She had Bob bring her a pair of trousers, a shirt, and a bandana.

"That's better," she nodded. "Now all I need is a **HORSE** and I'm ready for **ACTION!**"

Bob pointed to four horses in front of his store.

He piled other supplies on the counter. I counted four saddles, four blankets, four canteens, four bowls, four spoons, and far too many cans of baked beans. **Did I mention I have a sensitive stomach?**

My Cousin Will Pay!

"That's what you need, strangers," Bob said when he had gathered all our **SUPPLIES**. "Now, how will you be paying?"

Trap pointed to me. "**My cousin will pay!**" he squeaked.

I wasn't surprised. Trap loves spending money ... especially when it's mine.

I pulled out some notes from my wallet. Bob eyed them with **SUSPICION**.

"Never saw money like this," he said. "Nope, you need **GOLD** in these parts, stranger."

notes

With a sigh, I gave him my gold watch.

"**Not enough**, partner" he said, pocketing the watch. "I'll need more gold. What else do you have?"

gold watch

Before I could think, Trap spoke up. "My cousin has a gold tooth," he announced.

Bob took out a pair of pliers. **"Open up,"** he ordered.

gold tooth

CHEESE NIBBLETS! He was going to yank out my gold tooth! I felt faint.

Just then, my sister jumped to my rescue. **"Stop! Don't touch him!"** she shrieked. I've got lots of gold for you."

Good old Thea.

I watched as she plunked down all of her gold jewellery on the counter.

"Not enough!" Bob declared.

At that moment, Trap mumbled something under his breath. Then he pulled out a gold chain that was hidden under his shirt. On it hung a **GIANT SHINY LETTER T**.

We all stared at it. That T must have weighed a tonne.

Still Bob insisted it wasn't enough.

gold chain

I was getting **ANNOYED**. What more did this mouse want from us? Our firstborn mouselings?

It was time to put my paw down. Our gold was worth at least a few scruffy-looking horses. But before I could squeak, Benjamin piped up.

"Mr Bob, I don't have any **GOLD**," he began. "But maybe you'd like my new **Cheese Blaster 4000** game."

He pulled a small electronic video game from his backpack. Colourful pictures of Swiss slices and mozzarella balls zoomed across the screen.

Bob's eyes lit up like my grandfather **Cheap Mouse Willy's** when he discovers a penny on the pavement.

"You've got a deal!" he squeaked. "This toy is fabumouse!"

By now, it was already dusk. We gathered our supplies and took off.

We needed to find a place to spend the night. **But where?** Where do you spend the night in the Wild, Wild West?

Something told me there were no five-star Furtown Hotels in Cactus City.

Squeaky-Time Tea?

Just then we spotted a sign tacked to the front of the saloon. It read:

ROOMS FOR RENT!

Thea clapped her paws. "OK, everyone. Here's what we're going to do," she announced. "**Gerry Berry** will go into the saloon. He will book us two rooms for the night. The rest of us will take care of the horses."

One thing you should know about Thea – she loves being **THE BOSS**.

I stared at the noisy saloon. "Can't you come in with me?" I asked. I'm a little SHY in front of strangers.

Trap pushed me towards the door. "Oh, stop being such a scaredy-mouse," he snorted. "Shake a paw!"

I frowned. "**Don't push me!** I can't stand it when you push me!" I squeaked.

I stepped into the **SALOON**. Cowrats were everywhere. They were playing cards. They were flinging darts. They were picking their teeth with pocketknives. **RAT-MUNCHING RATTLESNAKES!** Those cowrats were tough!

THE SALOON

I listened to one rodent banging away at the piano. He was **awful**. But I didn't dare say a word. He might use me to pick his teeth!

Just then a mouse screeched at me from behind the bar.

"What d'ya want, stranger?" he yelled. My stomach was churning. I guessed it was the beans.

I decided a hot cup of ***Squeaky-Time Tea*** would be just perfect. So I asked him for one.

His mouth hit the floor. "Did you say a hot cup of ***Squeaky-Time Tea?***" he repeated.

I nodded. I wondered why he looked so surprised. I know the name sounds **silly**, but it really is a very soothing tea.

He snorted and turned to the crowd. "Did ya hear what the stranger wants to drink?" he bellowed. "Squeaky-Time Tea!"

The piano player stopped playing. Everyone turned towards me. They were *QUIET AS MICE*.

Then they started laughing. "Squeaky-Time Tea? **HA-HA-HAAA!!**"

The bartender slid a cup of tea down the counter towards me ... but I **MISSED**.

The crowd snickered.

The bartender threw me a second cup of tea ... but I missed again.

They all **GUFFAWED**.

The bartender threw me a third cup.

This time, I caught it on the fly.

It was my turn to sneer. So I did. Then I let out an ear-piercing scream.

The cup was scalding hot!

The bartender threw me a cup of tea ...

then a second cup of tea ...

... and a third! This time, I caught it on the fly!

Stranger, Cactus City Is Too Small for the Two Of Us!

I blew on my paws. They felt like they were on fire.

I started hopping around in a circle screaming, **"OUCH, OUCH, OUCH!"**

Then I heard a crunch. **Oops!** I had accidentally stepped on someone's paw.

I turned around. I was snout to snout with an ugly rat with **HUMONGOUS** muscles. Yikes!

"S-s-s-soorry," I stammered.

He gnashed his teeth. "You did that on purpose!" he roared.

Then he spat into a metal bucket across the room. Ping! **PERFECT SHOT**.

I turned PALE. "No, really, it was an accident," I tried to explain.

He didn't let me finish. "Stranger, Cactus City is too small for the two of us!" he declared.

I was shivering in my boots. **Oh, why did I have to step on this cowrat's toes?** He was bigger than a pro rat wrestler.

"Of course, I'll leave immediately," I muttered.

But the rodent held up his paw. "Too late, stranger," he squeaked. "No one messes with **MICK MUSCLE MOUSE**

and gets away with it. We need to fight it out. One of us will live, and the other will be **PUSHING UP DAISIES**."

The undertaker applauded. "Pushing up daisies. I like it!" He leaned out the door and yelled to the gravedigger. "Hey, Grimsly, get a **CASKET** ready!" he instructed. "On second thought, make that two caskets. We might get **lucky**!"

Then he looked me up and down. "So, stranger, what's your name?" he asked.

I gulped. "Well, my name is **GERONIMO**," I said.

G as in **GENTLE**.

E as in **EDUCATED**.

R as in **RESPECTFUL**.

O as in **OH**, I am so sorry that I stepped on Mick Muscle Mouse's paw!

N as in **NOT** done on purpose.

I as in **I** am a polite mouse.

M as in **MY**, oh, my, how did I ever get into this mess?

O as in **OH**, poor, poor me!

The undertaker chiselled my name on the coffin. "Um, let's see, that's **GERONIMO** ..."

G as in **GONNA** pay me in advance, while you're still breathing.

E as in **EVERYBODY** has to kick the bucket sooner or later.

R as in you **REALLY** blew it this time.

O as in **OH**, why did you stop in Cactus City?

N as in **NO** one lasts long here.

I as in **I** pity you ...

M as in **MAYBE** you'll tell me why you stepped on the foot of Mick Muscle Mouse, of all rodents?

O as in **OH**, well, hope you had a nice life!

Mick jumped to his paws. **"Let me at him!"** he shrieked. "I'll **FLATTEN** him! I'll mash him into cottage cheese! I'll skin him like a rat-fur rug! I'll spread him out like **CREAM CHEESE!**"

Yoo-Hoo!

At that moment, a voice sang out. "Yoo-hoo! Mick Muscle Mouse! How are you doing this morning?" it trilled.

Dolly Dandywhiskers
The Proprieter of the dress shop

A pretty blonde rodent with bright blue eyes stood in front of us. She was dressed all in **pink**, from her snout to her tail. In her paw she carried a pink umbrella.

It was **Miss Dolly Dandywhiskers**. She owned the Pretty Paws Dress Shop in town.

"Why, Miss Dolly," Mick gushed. "You're looking lovely today."

It was then that I noticed Mick's fur had turned **beetroot-red**. Was he coming down with something?

Rodent pox? The flu? A terrible case of sunburn? Then I realised he was beaming at Miss Dolly. I snickered. Yep, Mick Muscle Mouse was sick all right. He was **lovesick**!

Just then, Dolly dropped her tiny lace handkerchief on the ground.

Mick let go of my ear. He ***RAN*** to pick up Dolly's handkerchief.

Dolly smiled. "Oh, thank you so much, Mr Muscle Mouse," she gushed.

Mick grinned. I grinned, too. Not because those two were in love. But because Mick had completely forgotten about me!

I grabbed my tail and ran!

SAVED BY A WHISKER!

I searched all over for my family. But it was as if they had disappeared.

They were not in the **SALOON**.

They were not in the **GENERAL STORE**.

They were not at the **BLACKSMITH'S**.

They were not at the **doctor's**.

They were not at the **PRINTER'S**.

And they were not at the **school**. Although that last one didn't surprise me. My cousin Trap never did well in school. His best subject was lunch. Two cheese toasties + two Cheddar pies = one happy Trap.

Just then I heard someone shouting. It was my cousin. He was at the RAILWAY STATION.

Then I heard another voice. I gulped. It was Mick Muscle Mouse!

The two were arguing. It seemed that both wanted to use the same watering trough for their horses.

Trap's voice was loud and shrill. "You think you're so smart!" he shrieked. "Just wait till my cousin gets here! He'll **teach you** a thing or two. He's got more brains than a whole library!"

Mick spat on the ground. "Oh, yeah?" he thundered. "Who's your **cousin?**"

I tried pretending I was a statue. It didn't work. A plump rodent in the crowd spotted me.

"There he is, Mick! The one with the glasses!" he pointed out.

Trap pushed me forwards. I nearly fell flat on my snout.

"**Don't push me!** I can't stand it when you push me!" I complained.

Mick Muscle Mouse glared at me. "You again?" he yelled.

The next thing I knew, I was flying through the air. Mick had just hurled me into the sky. I landed with

You again?

a loud **SPLASH** in the watering trough. The horses looked annoyed.

The undertaker, on the other paw, looked **THRILLED**. He jumped up and down and clapped his paws. "Grimsly, let's finish that wooden **coffin** for the stranger!" he cried. "Something tells me he may need one soon!"

A coffin the perfect size for Geronimo!

Grimsly snickered and raced away.

Right at that moment, a skinny old lady with a flower in her hat came by. She reminded me of my great-aunt **No Nonsense**. She was one strict rodent.

"Mick Muscle Mouse!" I heard the old lady yell. "What are you doing?"

Mick looked at the ground. "N-n-nothing, Teacher," he stuttered.

She waved her cane in the air. "Very good, Mick," she squeaked. "Because I'm keeping my eye on you. And you'd better behave! Just because you're not in school anymore doesn't mean you can disobey the rules!"

Miss Firm Fur
The Teacher

Mick shuffled his paws. "Oh, of course, Miss Firm Fur," he mumbled.

As soon as she left, Mick looked for me. But as my cousin said, I'm one smart mouse. **I had already hightailed it out of there.**

No Guns For Geronimo Stilton

We returned to the saloon. Our rooms were on the first floor. The beds were full of **FLEAS**. The walls were **stained** and peeling. The floor had **mounds of dust**. And the smell was enough to drive a mouse to drink rat poison!

Trap pinched his nose. "**Germeister**, is that you? You should stay away from those beans!" he smirked.

I sighed. **Oh, why did I get stuck with such an obnoxious cousin?** He was so annoying. He was so immature. He was so ... clumsy.

I watched in **HORROR** as Trap threw open the shutters, knocking over a huge vase of flowers. It crashed down onto the street.

"**Be careeeeeeeful!** You could hit somebody!" I shrieked.

I scrambled to the window. **CHEESE NIBBLETS!** The vase had hit somebody. Mick Muscle Mouse stood under the window holding a flower. I could see a huge bump forming on his head.

"YOU AGAIN!" he roared. "Stranger, tonight I'm going to finish you off! I'm gonna send you packing! You'll be headed for the great big cheese deli in the sky!"

In a flash, the undertaker appeared next to him. "**BIG CHEESE DELI IN THE SKY?**" he squeaked, rubbing his paws together.

I ran down to the saloon. I had to straighten things out between Mick and me. After all, I never meant to upset anyone.

Unfortunately, Mick was another story. He loved hurting mice. And he was proud of it.

"Stranger! Tonight there'll be one less rodent in Cactus City! Get ready for a **SHOOT-OUT!**" he yelled.

My teeth began to chatter. "I will certainly n-n-n-not get r-r-r-ready f-f-f-for a shoot-out," I stammered. "Geronimo Stilton does not shoot g-g-g-guns."

Mick rolled his eyes. "This stranger is a scaredy-mouse!" he cried.

Everyone in the saloon stared at me. "SCAREDY-MOUSE! SCAREDY-MOUSE!" they chanted.

Squeaks of laughter filled my ears.

No guns for Geronimo Stilton!

I Did Not Do It on Purpose!

Before I could decide what to do next ...

1. I slipped on a potato peel.
2. I somersaulted into the air.
3. I accidentally kicked Mick in the snout.
4. I grabbed the chandelier.
5. I swung onto the balcony.
6. I slid down the banister.
7. I accidentally headbutted Mick.
8. I fell back on a loose board.
9. I knocked a watermelon into the air.
10. I watched the watermelon land on Mick's head.
11. "I did not do it on purpose!" I apologised to Mick.

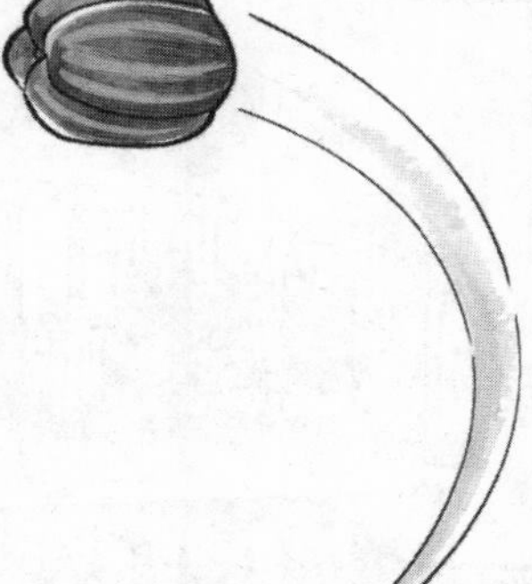

1 I slipped on a potato peel.

2 I somersaulted into the air.

3 I accidentally kicked Mick in the snout.

4 I grabbed the chandelier.

5 I swung onto the balcony.

6 I slid down the banister.

7 I accidentally headbutted Mick.

8 I fell back on a loose board.

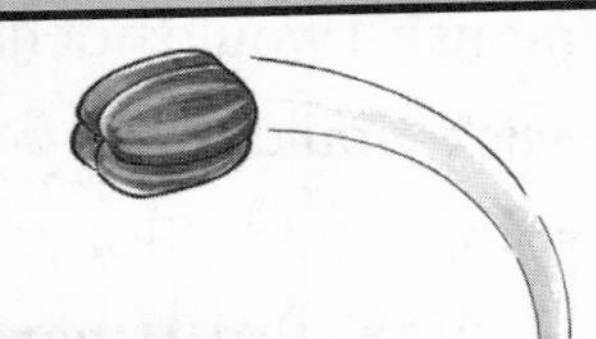

9 I knocked a watermelon into the air.

10 I watched the watermelon land on Mick's head.

11 I apologised to Mick.

The crowd in the saloon stared at me with respect. "What a mouse! What a fighter! **What a daredevil!**"

"But I did not do it on purpose! I am not a fighter! I'm not strong!" I protested.

Miss Firm Fur, the teacher felt my muscles. "Young mouse, I would not have bet a penny on you. I thought Mick would make **Swiss cheese** out of you," she commented. "But you are strong."

Miss Dolly batted her eyelashes. "Oooh, Mr Geronimo," she squeaked in a soft voice. "You are so much stronger than Mr Muscle Mouse. Much, Much **STRONGER!**"

I could tell Mick felt awful. He looked as if he were going to cry.

The undertaker scratched his head. "Too bad they didn't **FIGHT** it out," he sighed. "No coffins needed here, I guess."

At that moment the earth trembled.

A cloud of dust rolled into town. A group of **GUN-TOTING MICE** galloped behind it.

Someone in the crowd whispered, "The evil gunmice are coming!"

I looked around me. Everyone looked terrified. The doctor, the blacksmith, the teacher, the banker. **Yes, even Mick Muscle Mouse looked afraid.**

I Am the Strongest!

The **GUNMICE** stopped in the centre of town. They were pulling a wagon. Inside the wagon sat an **ENORMOUSE** barrel.

I wondered what was inside it. But there was no time to think about it. I was too busy thinking about the leader of the gunmice.

He was the **SCARIEST** rodent I had ever seen! He was dressed all in black from his leather trousers to his coal-black hat. His black **COWRAT** boots were extra pointy. They looked like they could spear a rodent with one hard paw-kick. His face seemed to be stuck in a permanent scowl. I *shivered*.

WICKED WHISKERS

Who was this evil gunmouse, and what was he doing in Cactus City?

Just then I noticed something shiny pinned to his shirt pocket. **RAT-MUNCHING RATTLESNAKES!** It was a **sheriff's star!** How could this evil-looking gunmouse be a sheriff?

A crowd gathered around him.

"Citizens of Cactus City!" the evil-looking gunmouse shouted. "From now on, you will **CHEER** when I enter town. I want **SINGING**. I want dancing. I want a plate of nachos with heaping **MOUNDS** of Cheddar!"

Rodents rushed to obey his orders. One led a chorus of **"Long Live the Sheriff!"** Another started teaching a new line dance. A third produced a plate of steaming nachos.

The sheriff shoved some nachos into his mouth. "Too hot, you **FOOL!**" he hissed.

Everyone stopped cheering. They stopped singing. They stopped dancing.

They were too scared to squeak.

Who Will Volunteer?

Then a voice rose up from the crowd. It was the old lady teacher, Miss Firm Fur.

"Citizens of Cactus City, you should be **ashamed** of yourselves!" she cried, waving her cane in the air. "This gunmouse is just a big old bully. Who will stand up to him? I need a strong **VOLUNTEER** to step forward."

Suddenly, someone pushed me from behind.

I should have known. It was my cousin Trap.

"**Don't push me!** I can't stand it when you push me!" I screeched.

Meanwhile, the **teacher** watched me with an approving eye. "Well done, stranger! I knew you were courageous. You are strong! Yes, you are very strong!" she said.

The crowd repeated, "The stranger is strong! He is very **STRONG!**" I turned pale. "But I am not strong, and I am not courageous, either," I tried to explain.

No one was listening.

"Come on, scaredy-mouse, don't embarrass the Stilton family!" Thea ordered.

I felt **FAINT**. I thought family was supposed to stick by you. But my family was trying to get me killed!

The gunmouse approached me. He took off his sunglasses and stuck his face close to mine. His eyes were as narrow as a killer cobra's.

My head began to pound. **Oh, how did I get myself into such a mess?**

"What's your name, stranger?" the gunmouse asked.

I told him. It wasn't easy. My teeth were chattering so hard, I felt like I was squeaking another language.

"My name is **WICKED WHISKERS**," the gunmouse snarled. "And I'm going to make you sorry you ever came to **Cactus City!**"

I gulped. I was already sorry. I was so sorry, I wanted to break into sobs, like a baby mouselet. But how could I? The citizens of Cactus City were counting on me.

"I challenge you to a rodeo at my ranch. Whoever can ride and tame **Bessie** wins!" the gunmouse declared. "If you win, I'll leave Cactus City forever."

I looked around me. The rodents of Cactus City were staring at me, **WORRIED**. I was their last hope. I had no choice.

I accepted the challenge. **After all, I told myself, how bad could an animal named Bessie be?**

Together, We Can Do Anything!

Wicked Whiskers held his paw in the air. The **EVIL** gunmice jumped back onto their horses. "See you at the ranch!" Wicked sneered at me. Then he left at a gallop.

I was **SEARED**. I didn't know anything about **RODEOS**. I am a city mouse.

The last time I rode a horse was on the mousey-go-round at the **Blue Cheese County Carnival**. I was dizzy for a week afterwards.

I hung my head.

Just then, someone tapped my shoulder. It was Mick Muscle Mouse. "Don't worry, stranger. I'll help you," he said. **"YOUR COURAGE IS CONTAGIOUS!"**

All the citizens of Cactus City clapped. "Your courage is contagious!" they cheered.

I smiled I didn't tell anyone I really was a scaredy-mouse. I needed all the help I could get.

"Don't forget us, **Gerry Berry**!" Thea called. Trap and Benjamin nodded.

"Together, we can do anything!" they shouted.

I was feeling a lot better. I was happy my family was behind me. They really can be great when they want to be. **Now if I could just get my sister to stop calling me Gerry Berry ....**

Wicked Whiskers' Water Dam

Before I went to the evil gunmouse's ranch, I needed to know more about him. Mick told me the whole **sad story**.

It seemed Wicked Whiskers was the owner of a piece of land north of **Cactus City**. A river ran through the land. For years, the river ran straight to Cactus City and was used for farming, cattle, and the citizens of the town. Then Wicked decided he wanted to control Cactus City. He built a **DAM** so the water no longer reached the city. Fields got dry. Cattle got THIRSTY.

"Now we have to pay Wicked to deliver water to us," Mick explained with a sigh. "He makes us pay for the water in **GOLD**."

I was disgusted. What kind of mouse would steal water from needy rodents? It was sneaky. It was cruel.

It was **ENOUGH** to make me ready to take on Wicked Whiskers.

Mick showed me a map. "We'll need three days and three nights to reach the **BIG W**, Wicked Whiskers' ranch," he said.

Thea, Trap and Benjamin were excited.

"This is going to be **fabumouse!**" Thea cheered.

"We'll be like real **cowrats!**" Trap grinned.

"I love **HORSES!**" Benjamin squeaked.

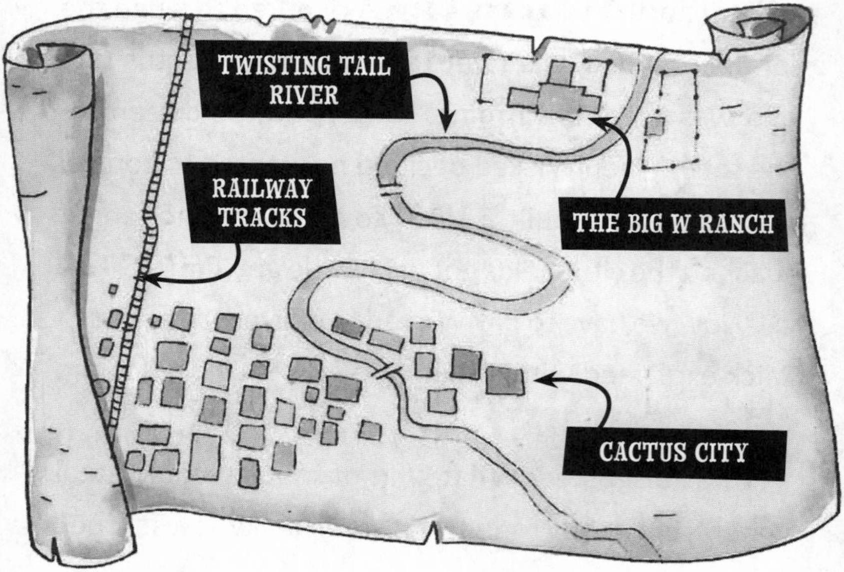

I felt limp. I couldn't **ride a horse** for three days. I didn't even know how.

Before I could protest, Mick threw me on a horse. It took off at a **GALLOP**.

I hung on for dear life. One minute, I was hanging **UPSIDE DOWN** from the saddle. The next minute, I was facing the horse's tail.

The crowd watched me go. "Look at the stranger! He's a regular gymnast!" I heard one mouse cry.

"I've never seen anything like it!" another added.

"He's better than a circus acrobat!" someone else squeaked.

I tried not to sob hysterically. **I didn't want to upset the good rodents of Cactus City.**

Streams, Snakes and Scorpions

We galloped for hours and hours under the sun.

We passed by **THE GRAND CANYON**. I stopped at the edge and looked below. Have you ever been to the Grand Canyon? It is **UNBELIEVABLE!** I had always thought the canyon was formed by very high mountains, but it is not.

THE GRAND CANYON is located in Arizona. It is a series of gorges carved by the Colorado River flowing through it for thousands and thousands of years. It is 1,828 metres deep, 354 kilometres long, and from 5 to 29 kilometres wide.

It grew cold as night fell. I couldn't stop shivering. We decided to rest.

We finally sat around the **FIRE**. Trap played on the banjo. Mick played the harmonica. Then we all sang **'Oh! Susannah.'** I have to admit, it was a lot of fun!

Oh! Susannah:

I come from Alabama
With my banjo on my knee,
I'm going to Louisiana,
My true love for to see.
It rained all night
The day I left,
The weather it was dry,
The sun so hot,
I froze to death,
Susannah, don't you cry.
Oh! Susannah,
Don't you cry for me
For I come from Alabama
With my banjo on my knee.

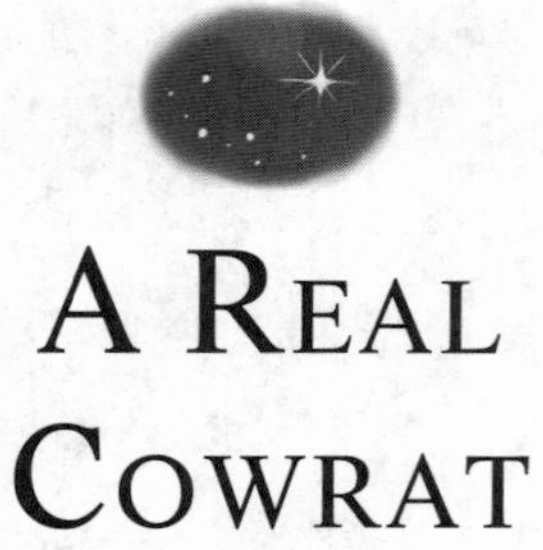

A Real Cowrat

That night I fell asleep next to my **FRIENDS**. I was wrapped in a warm blanket, with my head resting on my saddle. Before I drifted off, I gazed up into the sky. Thousands and thousands of stars kept watch over me.

It was an amazing sight.

In the morning, I nibbled on a **TASTY** breakfast – a stack of yummy Cheddar pancakes, bacon, an egg, and two slices of American cheese toast. It was **whisker-licking** good!

I was feeling great. I always do when my belly is full of cheese. Plus, I was getting used to being on a horse. Mick taught me how to use a **LASSO**. He explained why a horse needs shoes, when to brush it and how to feed it.

I galloped across the plains with the wind whipping through my whiskers. **CHEESECAKE**, I was having fun! I felt like a real cowrat.

Yes, I, Geronimo "Scaredy-Mouse" Stilton, was beginning to really like the **WILD, WILD WEST!**

EVERYTHING ON HORSES!

Most horses today live in stables and are used to a tame way of living. It is their nature to live in freedom, but most would find it difficult to readjust to the wild life of the old West.

Horses live in stalls spacious enough to allow them to move and to rest. The stalls are dry and well ventilated, and the floor should be covered with straw for the horses to rest on.

Horses need to eat several meals a day. Their food should be placed inside their stalls, near their water. Besides hay and fresh grass, a horse's diet consists of oats, apples and carrots.

Horses are very clean animals. They like to be curried (brushed) once a day. This is good for their coats because it removes loose hair and dirt.

A horse gets new shoes every thirty-five to forty days. A horse's hooves are thick but need to be protected by metal shoes. A person who shoes horses is called a blacksmith or a farrier. The farrier removes the old shoes, then cuts and files the hooves and attaches a new pair of shoes.

A Nightmare Named ... Bessie!

We finally arrived at Wicked Whiskers' **RANCH**. It was dark and spooky-looking. The whole place made my fur **CRAWL**.

Just then Wicked sauntered up. "Are you ready to lose, stranger? Are you ready to face **Bessie?**" he cackled.

I tried to look **TOUGH**, but inside I felt like a bowl of cream cheese and jam.

"N-n-no p-p-p-problem," I stammered. I closed my eyes and took a **DEEP BREATH**. How bad could an animal named Bessie be?

Then I saw him. Bessie, I mean. He was an immense black **BEAST** the size of two double-decker cheese delivery trucks. He had terrifying red eyes that looked like they were on fire. His horns were as long as my tail.

My eyes nearly popped out of my fur. No, Bessie wasn't dangerous. He was **DEADLY!**

"W-w-what is that?" I croaked.

Trap snorted. "Wake up and smell the cheese, **Germeister**," he scoffed. "It's a bull, of course. Look at those horns! One poke and you'll run squeaking for your life!"

I felt **FAINT**. No wonder Wicked Whiskers knew he would win the challenge. I'd never be able to ride Bessie. Not for all the **Cheesy Chews** in the world!

"Go, cousin, move your tail!" Trap ordered. Then he pushed me.

"**Don't push me!** I can't stand it when you push me!" I grabbed the fence. "I changed my mind. I can't do this!" I squeaked.

Thea rolled her eyes. "Oh, don't be such a **crybaby** mouse," she groaned.

So much for her support, I steamed.

A little paw grabbed mine. "Uncle Geronimo, you can do it. I have **faith** in you!" little Benjamin whispered.

Of course, that's all it took. How could I let my dear sweet nephew down? I could hear Bessie snorting in his pen. He's not angry, I told myself. He's just got a bad cold.

With SHAKY paws, I climbed onto his back.

The door of the pen opened.

Bessie took off like a shot!

"Goodbye, Stiltons! Goodbye, Mick! Goodbye, rodents everywhere!" I sobbed.

WHY, WHY, WHY?

I tried to hold on to Bessie, but he was too **STRONG** for me. In a flash, he'd thrown me to the ground.

"Help!" I squeaked as Bessie tried to trample me. I was able to get away but he was right on my tail. His horns hooked my shirt. He **TOSSED** me into the air. I bounced off the fence. Then I landed back on Bessie.

He was yelling horn ...

or was it corn?

Suddenly, I spotted my little nephew Benjamin. He was waving his paw frantically. What was he trying to tell me? Benjamin started yelling something. It sounded like **HORN**. Or was that **CORN?**

Next, my nephew began pointing at his ear. Did he have an **EARACHE?**

He pointed at his ear.

I love my nephew, but I couldn't worry about his ears right now.

Just then I glanced down at Bessie's **MASSIVE** neck. That's when I noticed his ear. A huge cactus thorn was stuck on it. **HOLEY CHEESE!** So that's what my nephew was trying to tell me The thorn was making Bessie hopping mad. As I tumbled off his back, I plucked the thorn from his ear.

Bessie stopped snorting. He stopped kicking. He stopped moving. He laid his head on my shoulder. And then he **smiled**. I patted his head and jumped on his back. I couldn't believe it. I, Geronimo Stilton, had **TAMED** Bessie!

Benjamin ran toward me.

"You saved my life, nephew!" I squeaked. I pulled him up onto Bessie's back. We took a **VICTORY LAP** around the ranch.

The rodents of Cactus City arrived. **They clapped and cheered us on.**

I jumped on the bull ...

He threw me off ...

He almost trampled me ...

He chased after me ...

He butted me
with his horns ...

I flew through
the air ...

I bounced off the fence ...

I landed back on Bessie!

I plucked the thorn ...

I patted his head ...

I landed back on Bessie!

Strong Rodents Know How to Forgive!

Meanwhile, Wicked Whiskers was **FURIOUS**, He couldn't understand why **Bessie** wasn't mad anymore.

"Why didn't you make cream cheese out of the stranger?" he screamed at the bull. "My grandma WIMPY WHISKERS is tougher than you!"

Bessie stamped his hoof. With a snort, he tossed Wicked Whiskers into the air.

The gunmouse fell to the ground. The bull put his hoof on Whiskers' tummy.

Wicked Whiskers' teeth were chattering. His tail was twitching. "D-d-d-don't hurt m-m-m-me!" the gunmouse stammered.

Stop, Bessie!
I'm sorry!

I knelt down next to Wicked Whiskers. The crowd gathered around.

"I think you owe the citizens of **Cactus City** an apology," I said. "You need to give them back their water. You need to stop being a **BULLY**."

The gunmouse nodded his head.

"You are right, stranger," he whispered. "I'm sorry for what I've done."

But the crowd wasn't convinced.

"Let's make him **pay for it!**" a mouse screeched.

"Let's get even!" another shouted.

I knew I had to do something quick. "Violence is not the answer," I told the citizens of Cactus City. "Strong rodents know how to **forgive**. You need to show Wicked Whiskers you are stronger than he is. You need to let him go."

The crowd stopped yelling. They looked embarrassed.

I patted the bull's head. Then I told him to take his hoof off Wicked Whiskers. He did.

Wicked let out a sigh of relief. "Thanks, stranger," he grinned. "You really are a **STRONG** cowrat!"

He took off his sheriff's star. Then he jumped on his horse. **His gunmice followed. They galloped off, leaving behind a cloud of dust.**

Yippee!

After the gunmice left, we went to the **Twisting Tail River.** We found the dam that kept the water from reaching Cactus City. It had a handle that locked.

"Geronimo, you unlock that thing," Thea ordered. "Then, Mick, you pull it out. OK, let's go! **Go! Go!**"

Minutes later, the dam was open. Water flowed out with a loud **WHOOSH**.

"Yippee!" we shouted.

Thea and Trap did a dance. Benjamin clapped his paws. And Mick let out a happy whistle.

As for me, I pulled out a tin cup from my supplies. I knelt down and scooped up some water from the river. **I don't know about everyone else, but I was dying of thirst!**

The dam was open!

A Tin Star in Search of a Sheriff

Back in Cactus City, the judge held a meeting.

"This tin star is in search of a **SHERIFF**," he announced. "We need a **STRONG** cowrat to defend our rights".

The rodents of Cactus City nodded. Just then a schoolmouse ran over to me.

"The stranger is a strong cowrat," he said. "He could be our new sheriff." He placed the **TIN STAR** in my paw.

I knew that I couldn't stay in Cactus City. After all, I had a newspaper to run back home. And what about my subscription to the **Cheese-of-the-Month Club?** I couldn't let all that good food go to waste.

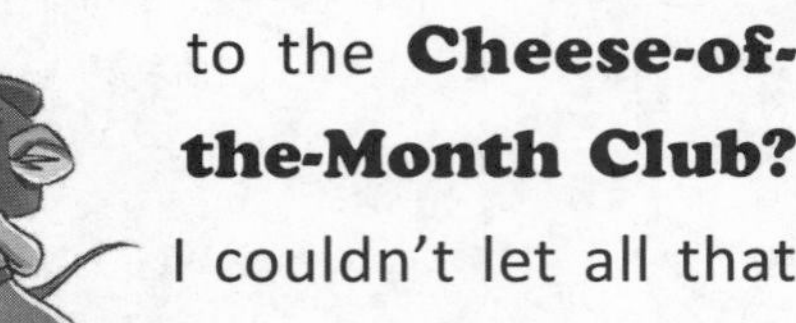

"Why don't you choose our new sheriff," the judge suggested.

I looked around at the crowd. Everyone was quiet. They were waiting. Waiting for me to make a decision. My head started **POUNDING**. I hate being put on the spot. What if I made a mistake? What if everyone **LAUGHED** at me? What if I had permanent hat fur when I left Cactus City? But that was another story. There wasn't time to worry about it now.

At that moment, I spotted Mick Muscle Mouse. I grinned. Mick was the **PERFECT** mouse for the job. He was strong. He was brave. He knew right from wrong.

I threw the star to Mick. He caught it in midair.

"You are the perfect **SHERIFF** for this city, friend," I said.

Tears sprang to Mick's eyes. Anyone could see he was a big mouse with a **big heart**. "I'll do my best to earn your respect," Mick said to the crowd.

Everyone **CHEERED**.

Suddenly, a swirling cloud of dust enveloped me. My head started spinning. My heart started racing. What was happening? I felt like I was flying, but I wasn't sitting in a cosy seat watching a film. I wasn't even on an aeroplane! **I let out a scream.**

AAAAAAAAAHHHHHHH!!!!

Where Am I?

I woke up **STARTLED**.

"Where am I?" I mumbled.

I looked around.

I was in my room.

In my **home**.

In New Mouse City!

No, I was not in the **WILD WEST** after all. It was only a dream.

I heard a droning sound.

The TV was on.

Then I remembered something. I had been watching television before I fell asleep. **I was watching an adventure story about the Wild, Wild West!**

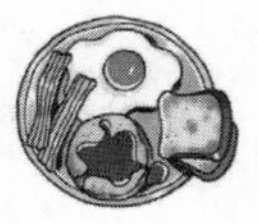

'Oh! Susannah'

I shuffled to the bathroom. I looked for a **pail** so I could wash my face.

Then I remembered ... I wasn't in the Wild West.

I looked for a pail.

I went down to the kitchen for breakfast. I looked for a **can of beans** to eat.

Then I remembered ... I wasn't in the Wild West.

I went outside. I looked for my **HORSE** to ride to work.

Then I remembered ... I wasn't in the Wild West anymore.

I looked for my horse.

At last I realised what was happening.

I was **missing** the Wild West. I wanted to go back – for real.

I took a taxi to the office. I hummed 'Oh! Susannah' as we zoomed along. It seemed as if there were a thousand cars on the street. Rodents beeped. Brakes screeched. What a **RAT RACE!** I needed a break.

That's when I got an idea. No, not just any idea. A great, perfect, fabumouse idea!

I raced up the stairs of The Rodent's Gazette. I called Thea, Trap, and Benjamin into my office.

"I feel like taking a trip," I announced. "Who wants to go with me to the **WILD, WILD WEST?**"

Of course, everyone wanted to go. My family loves to travel. And they love adventure.

Trap pushed me towards the door. "Good for you, **Germeister**!" he chuckled. "It's about time you stopped being a scaredy-mouse. You're gonna love the Wild, Wild West!"

I rolled my eyes. But then I smiled. I had to admit, for once, I knew my cousin was right.

Now if I could just get him to stop calling me Germeister ...

ABOUT THE AUTHOR

Born in New Mouse City, Mouse Island, GERONIMO STILTON is Rattus Emeritus of Mousomorphic Literature and of Neo-Ratonic Comparative Philosophy. For the past twenty years, he has been running The Rodent's Gazette, New Mouse City's most widely read daily newspaper.

Stilton was awarded the Ratitzer Prize for his scoops on *The Curse of the Cheese Pyramid* and *The Search for Sunken Treasure*. He has also received the Andersen Prize for Personality of the Year. His works have been published all over the globe.

In his spare time, Mr. Stilton collects antique cheese rinds and plays golf. But what he most enjoys is telling stories to his nephew Benjamin.

The Rodent's Gazette

1. Main entrance
2. Printing presses (where everything is printed)
3. Accounts department
4. Editorial room (where editors, illustrators, and designers work)
5. Geronimo Stilton's office
6. Geronimo's botanical garden

9
18
1
2
4
8
3
12
13
11
10
32
19
22
5
46
45
20
15
17
40
7
24
26
25
28
33
14
16
38
27
36
23
37
31
21
29
35
44
41
30
34
6
42
39
43

MAP OF NEW MOUSE CITY

1. Industrial Zone
2. Cheese Factories
3. Angorat International Airport
4. WRAT Radio and Television Station
5. Cheese Market
6. Fish Market
7. Town Hall
8. Snotnose Castle
9. The Seven Hills of Mouse Island
10. Mouse Central Station
11. Trade Centre
12. Movie Theatre
13. Gym
14. Catnegie Hall
15. Singing Stone Plaza
16. The Gouda Theatre
17. Grand Hotel
18. Mouse General Hospital
19. Botanical Gardens
20. Cheap Junk for Less (Trap's store)
21. Parking Lot
22. Mouseum of Modern Art
23. University and Library
24. The Daily Rat
25. The Rodent's Gazette
26. Trap's House
27. Fashion District
28. The Mouse House Restaurant
29. Environmental Protection Centre
30. Harbour Office
31. Mousidon Square Garden
32. Golf Course
33. Swimming Pool
34. Blushing Meadow Tennis Courts
35. Curlyfur Island Amusement Park
36. Geronimo's House
37. Historic District
38. Public Library
39. Shipyard
40. Thea's House
41. New Mouse Harbour
42. Luna Lighthouse
43. The Statue of Liberty
44. Hercule Poirat's Office
45. Petunia Pretty Paws's House
46. Grandfather William's House

MAP OF MOUSE ISLAND

1. Big Ice Lake
2. Frozen Fur Peak
3. Slipperyslopes Glacier
4. Coldcreeps Peak
5. Ratzikistan
6. Transratania
7. Mount Vamp
8. Roastedrat Volcano
9. Brimstone Lake
10. Poopedcat Pass
11. Stinko Peak
12. Dark Forest
13. Vain Vampires Valley
14. Goosebumps Gorge
15. The Shadow Line Pass
16. Penny-Pincher Castle
17. Nature Reserve Park
18. Las Ratayas Marinas
19. Fossil Forest
20. Lake Lake
21. Lake Lakelake
22. Lake Lakelakelake
23. Cheddar Crag
24. Cannycat Castle
25. Valley of the Giant Sequoia
26. Cheddar Springs
27. Sulphurous Swamp
28. Old Reliable Geyser
29. Vole Vale
30. Ravingrat Ravine
31. Gnat Marshes
32. Munster Highlands
33. Mousehara Desert
34. Oasis of the Sweaty Camel
35. Cabbagehead Hill
36. Rattytrap Jungle
37. Rio Mosquito
38. Mousefort Beach
39. San Mouscisco
40. Swissville
41. Cheddarton
42. Mouseport
43. New Mouse City
44. Pirate Ship of Cats

4
3
2
44
1
7
6
5
40
14
8
25
13
9
11
12
10
42
41
21
15
20
22
39
23
17
32
26
19
16
35
18
29
24
43
28
38
30
27
36
31
33
37
34

THE COLLECTION

HAVE YOU READ ALL OF GERONIMO'S ADVENTURES?

- ☐ *Lost Treasure of the Emerald Eye*
- ☐ *The Curse of the Cheese Pyramid*
- ☐ *Cat and Mouse in a Haunted House*
- ☐ *I'm Too Fond of My Fur!*
- ☐ *Four Mice Deep in the Jungle*
- ☐ *Paws Off, Cheddarface!*
- ☐ *Fangs and Feasts in Transratania*
- ☐ *Attack of the Pirate Cats*
- ☐ *A Fabumouse Holiday for Geronimo*
- ☐ *Hang on to Your Whiskers*
- ☐ *School Trip to Niagara Falls*
- ☐ *The Christmas Toy Factory*

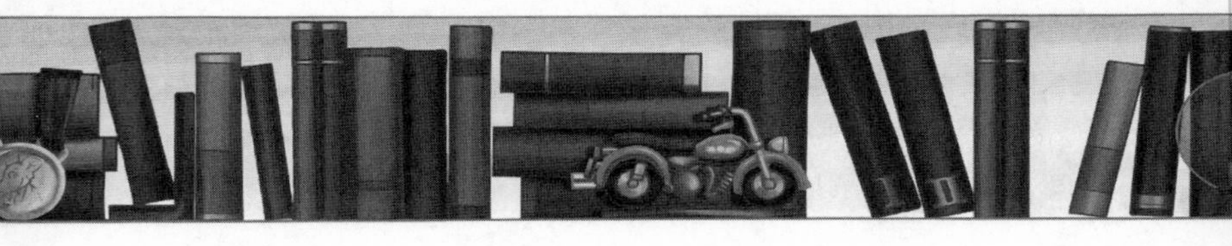

- ☐ *Geronimo Stilton, Secret Agent*
- ☐ *A Fantastic School Adventure*
- ☐ *The Cheese Experiment*
- ☐ *The Super Chef Contest*
- ☐ *Welcome to Mouldy Manor*
- ☐ *The Treasure of Easter Island*
- ☐ *Mouse Overboard!*
- ☐ *This Hotel Is Haunted*
- ☐ *A Cheese-Coloured Camper Van*
- ☐ *The Search for Sunken Treasure*
- ☐ *The Ghost of the Underground*
- ☐ *The Mona Mousa Code*
- ☐ *Surf's Up, Geronimo!*
- ☐ *The Mystery of the Roaring Rat*
- ☐ *Merry Christmas, Geronimo!*
- ☐ *Shipwreck on Pirate Island*

- ☐ *The Temple of the Fire Ruby*
- ☐ *The Mouse Island Marathon*
- ☐ *Valentine's Day Disaster*
- ☐ *Magical Mission*
- ☐ *Down and Out Down Under*
- ☐ *The Mummy with No Name*
- ☐ *The Way of the Samurai*
- ☐ *Valley of the Giant Skeletons*
- ☐ *A Very Merry Christmas*
- ☐ *The Wild, Wild West*
- ☐ *Operation: Secret Recipe*
- ☐ *The Race Across America*

HAPPY READING!